The Deer and the Snail

by Maureen Tai
Illustrated by Marcela Calderón

OXFORD
UNIVERSITY PRESS

adult

Once there was a little mouse deer called Sang Kancil. She was very small. Luckily, she was also very clever. She had to be clever to protect herself from other animals who wanted to eat her. However, she was also proud and boastful.

"I am the cleverest animal in this rainforest," the mouse deer announced loudly. "I am also the quickest!"

Being clever helped to protect Sang Kancil from other animals. What things might she have done to keep herself safe?

child

Snail was resting on a twig near Deer.

crunch, crunch

When you <u>announce</u> something, you say it loudly so everyone can hear. Can you <u>announce</u> that you are the fastest animal in the rainforest, just like Sang Kancil?

child

"You are not as quick as me!" said Snail. "I am *much* quicker!" Deer said. "I can run down the track quicker than you."

"I need a little nap," grunted Snail. "We can run soon."

child

adult

Snail didn't nap. Instead, he gathered his family together, including his brother, sister and three children. It was hard to tell them apart because they all looked alike.

"To <u>complete</u> the race, we must work as a team. You must all pretend to be me," Snail said. "One of you wait at the starting line. The rest of you, hide behind a bush at each bend of the track. When you hear Sang Kancil coming, slide out. I'll wait by the tree at the end of the track." Snail began to chuckle. "<u>Imagine</u> her surprise when I win!"

Can you <u>imagine</u> what Sang Kancil would look like if she thought Snail had beaten her in the race? Can you show what her surprised face might look like?

child

A big crowd started to gather at the track. "Stand there," Frog said to Deer and Snail. "Now, GO!"

Complete means to finish something. Who do you think will complete the race first, the snails or Sang Kancil?

child

Deer shot off. When she got to the bend, one of Snail's children crept out.

child

Deer spotted the snail. She had a shock! Deer ran quicker.

adult

At the second bend, Snail's sister slid out from a bush, shouting, "I'm already here!"

At the next bend, it was Snail's brother who crept out. "What's taking you so long?" he called.

Poor Sang Kancil was <u>confused</u>. However fast she ran, Snail was always ahead of her!

Sang Kancil is <u>confused</u> because she doesn't understand what's going on. Can you explain what's happening with the snails in the story?

child

Deer was getting cramp in her legs. They hurt!

child

Snail was near the end of the track.

child

He crept up to the finish.
Snail was the winner!

adult

Snail beamed with <u>delight</u> as his family came up the track. Sang Kancil realized she had been tricked. She didn't feel that clever or fast after all.

"I'm sorry I was so boastful," she said, hanging her head with shame.

"Now that you have said sorry, we will not play any more tricks on you," Snail said kindly.

Snail smiled with <u>delight</u> because he was very happy. Can you make a face as if you were smiling with <u>delight</u>?

"Deer?" Snail said.
Deer just grunted. She was asleep!

child

adult

Retell the story